This book belongs to:

....

AUTUMN
PUBLISHING

Written by Suzanne Fossey
Illustrated by Gina Maldonado
Designed by Lee Italiano
Edited by Suzanne Fossey

Published in 2021
First published in the UK by Autumn Publishing
An imprint of Igloo Books Ltd
Cottage Farm, NN6 0BJ, UK
Owned by Bonnier Books
Sveavägen 56, Stockholm, Sweden

Manufactured in China. 1121 005
10 9 8 7 6 5 4 3

Library of Congress Cataloging-in-Publication
Data is available upon request.

ISBN 978-1-83852-399-2
autumnpublishing.co.uk
bonnierbooks.co.uk

I was born in winter, in a warm and cozy den. I snoozed all through the snowy months 'til springtime came again.

I nudged my mom awake by **jumping** on her side.

**"Come on, Mommy, let's get up.
I want to go outside!"**

With sunlight streaming all around, the forest felt so bright!
The spiky grass tickled my paws
and I giggled with delight.

The flowers were so **pretty**
and the trees **stretched** up so high.

I tried to chase a butterfly as it came swooping by.

Mommy showed me how to dig
for tasty bugs and roots.

She even **pulled** a tree branch **down**
so I could try the **shoots**.

I chatted with a wise old owl,
whose laugh was like a squawk,

and met a massive moose,
who didn't want to talk.

I saw a small, red fox,
who invited me to play.

I said **hello** to all the birds,
but they just flew away.

At last we reached a valley and a swiftly flowing stream.
Around it were a HUNDRED bears, more than I'd ever seen.

"Can I go in the water, Mom? I want to run and play!"
"Yes, little one," she smiled at me. "But don't go far away."

I tried to be like bigger bears

and catch myself a fish,

but I missed my footing, slipped—

and **fell in**
with a
'Splish!"

I climbed up on the bank,
my fur all dripping wet.

"Don't be sad," said Mommy.

"You'll get that fishy yet."

Once we'd had our fill of fish,
we went back to the trees.

I found a hive I couldn't reach,
and lots of buzzing bees.

But as the summer came and went, I grew taller all the time.

Then, one day I stretched up tall, and the honey was all mine!

"Hello there," said the fox.
"Haven't you grown tall?"

"I have!" I said with a smile.
"It's nice to not be small."

"Oh, there's nothing wrong with being small," Fox said with a frown.

"No one pays attention when things are too far down."

Mommy said, "It's winter soon.
We need to find a den.

A **cozy** place to sleep
until the **spring**
comes back again."

I helped my mom to dig a hole just big enough to share.

We snuggled in together. "Sleep well, my little . . .

..bear!"

Bear cubs
are born in the winter
and sleep until springtime.
When they wake up, the mom and cub
leave the den and spend all summer and
fall looking for food. They meet other bears
and the cub learns to play, growing bigger and
stronger. When winter comes again, the mommy
bear shows the cub how to look for a new
den, and when the den is ready,
they curl up together and
fall asleep until the
next spring.